BROKEN HOME,
HEALED NEST

T0349362

BROKEN HOME,
HEALED NEST

PERSHLIE "PERCI" AMI
ANTHONY GOULET

Broken Home, Healed Nest

Cover Art: Eloy Bida
Editor: Lisa Frenette
Proofreader: Patricia Robertson

ISBN: 9781778540578
Published in Canada by Medicine Wheel Publishing
For more book information, please go to
www.medicinewheelpublishing.com

10   9   8   7   6   5   4   3   2   1

Printed in PRC

Funded by the   Financé par le
Government   gouvernement   Canada
of Canada   du Canada

Contents

Dear Friends & Relatives

This book deals with the subject of suicide. Suicide is a delicate topic. But suicide isn't just a topic, is it? It's a reality that affects far too many of us.

There are many kinds of tears, each holding their own emotion. Worlds within worlds, all with the potential to purify us as long as we don't allow them to drown us. Jessica is walking within a sadness of tears that are beginning to drown out the teachings she was always able to use as her life raft. Beautiful teachings through stories, songs, laughter and memories she courageously allowed to carry her through storm after storm, back to the calm, still waters of her heart. We all forget sometimes. And sometimes when we forget, the distance we feel from ourselves can be frightening.

What Jessica is going through is no ordinary storm. She has been holding on through many challenges for a long time. And perhaps you have, too. So, we ask you to please hold on and see where Jessica's journey goes, where it takes you. As you walk with her, please remember, no matter how challenging things may be for you in this moment, it is only a moment in your life, not your entire life, and certainly not the rest of your life.

We are grateful you are here. You are important. You matter. We need you.

If you need or want to speak with someone, please reach out to your safe community supports. And if you're not comfortable reaching out to your community for support, please call the number below where you can talk or text with someone twenty-four hours a day, seven days a week.

In both the United States and Canada, call or text 988 to reach the 988 Suicide & Crisis Lifeline. Trained counselors are available to speak with you 24/7.

Love,

Pershlie "Perci" Ami & Anthony Goulet

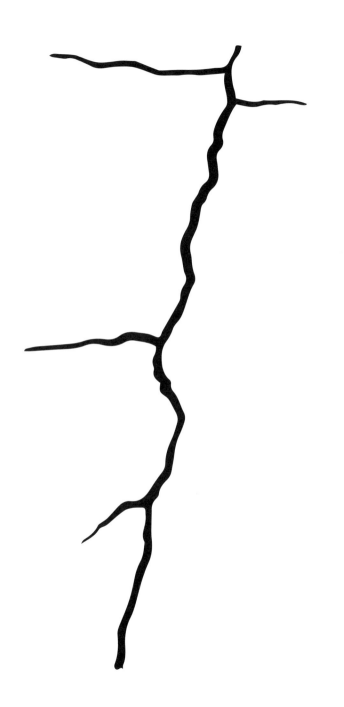

Chapter 1
Broken Home

God, I hate being woke up with the sounds of my parents yelling and glass breaking. I should probably go out to the kitchen and try to stop them. No, wait. The last time I did that their fighting came into my room. Yeah, that's right, that's why my window is still covered in cardboard. Oh no, they're going out in the front yard. The police are going to be here any minute now. Shit, this is crazy.

I know the neighbors can hear the chaos when my parents keep it inside, but it seems like they only call the cops when it's something they're forced to see. Maybe it disrupts their night, or maybe others just don't give a shit unless it's about to affect their lives. I don't have time for this, and I really don't care anymore. If my parents want to kill each other, fine, there's nothing I can do about that. I know the deal though: the cops will be here, they'll call Child Protective Services, arrest one or both of them, and off I'll go to the emergency shelter and maybe a temporary foster home. I'm tired of talking with police officers, social workers, CPS, and my parents. I'm tired of living like this.

I've spent years taking the advice of some family members, school counselors, the staff at the after-school program, and the spiritual leaders in the community. I'm fifteen years old now and spent the first twelve years of my life holding on and using my parents as teachers of how *not* to be. I held on as long as I could—through the screams, insanity, ambulances and police cars in our driveway, and many nights where I cried myself to sleep, begging the Creator to change things in my family. If the pillow I used from the time I was born until I was twelve years old could talk, it would tell you about all my tears, fears, and anguished screams to the Creator about my life.

I've spent so many nights in hospital waiting rooms, rehab visiting rooms, and other cold, sterile places with strangers asking me personal questions about me and my family. What bothered me more was when those strangers would come inside our home and ask me personal questions, because it made me feel like our home wasn't our home anymore. There's a way to enter someone's home, you know. You always enter another person's home with respect. My grandmother taught me that. She taught me so many things. Maybe what angered me is that the strangers would refer to our home as a home, when for so long I never felt like it was. Some of the strangers were tribal members, others weren't, but one word they all used was the word *help*. I learned at an early age that what *help* means to me isn't what it means to other people. Besides, I never knew what someone could do to help, I just knew that I wanted to feel the way my grandmother made me feel. And until I was twelve years old, my grandmother is who the strangers would always call to pick me up and take me with her. Then she passed away, and when she did, I said those two magic words that all people say when their heart finally shatters after holding on for so long: I said *fuck it* and I meant it.

Yeah, I experimented with alcohol and drugs while my grandmother was still alive. She even caught me smoking weed once, and man, I felt ashamed, but she told me to never feel ashamed. She told me to never be ashamed of who I am. My grandmother would always say, "No matter what you think, say or do, I will always see, hear, believe and accept you as the sacred blessing, miracle and gift the Creator has created you as. I will always accept you, but that doesn't mean I will accept unacceptable behavior, so leave the drugs outside our home, come inside, and let's have some good food and conversation."

Her unconditional love and acceptance of me is what stopped me from saying *fuck it* years before she passed away. When she passed away, I lost the one person who, no matter what, celebrated me, accepted me, and made me feel as if there was absolutely nothing wrong with me. After she passed away, I went all in, all in to anything and everything that would make me feel good, even if it was just for a moment. And for the past three years since my grandmother passed away, I have been labeled as many things. Things like drug user, alcoholic, gang member, violent, at-risk, rude, disrespectful, delinquent, and whatever else they say. Most of the people who say those things know nothing about me. Hell, most of the people who say those things never even talked with me.

They just talk at me, letting me know that I'll be dead or in prison before I'm eighteen years old or some other dumb shit like that. Well, you know what? They can be right, because getting high and drunk is old now. It seems that I get drunk or high just to feel normal because the high, the buzz, has worn off. And getting into fights isn't exciting anymore. I think that fighting spirit within me is gone. The truth is … well, I don't know what the truth is, but I do know I'm tired of living.

I'm fifteen years old and already tired of living. Maybe because I haven't lived yet, just trudging my way through systems of hypocrisy, and promises that some would say are empty. But I don't think they are. The promises are full, and at the moment they're given I am filled with hope, and I rise. Hope makes you rise, but I'm tired of the fall. Beautiful balloons of hope, taking me high enough to see things from a different perspective, yet high enough to kill me when the hope deflates and I come crashing to the ground. Promises full of the hope of change, but none have ever lasted for more than a week. I've listened with hope as my parents promised, "We're so sorry. It won't happen again. Things are going to be different."

Like most kids, I'm forgiving and can go with the flow, even better than most adults. For how long though? Like the broken-down, abandoned car my dad bought when I was born. It's a 1957 Mercury. He showed me pictures of how it's going to look after he and I fully restore it. And he says that he wants to give it to me when I turn sixteen. He wanted it to be a father-daughter project that we would work on over the years. We've never worked on it together. The closest we came to working on it was when my mom was in rehab for a couple of months and my dad was going to Alcoholic Anonymous meetings. During that time, my dad had an AA sponsor who came over quite a bit and encouraged him. I guess my dad told him about the car and our father-daughter project because one day the AA guy brought over some of the materials my dad and I needed to begin restoring the car. Oh, I was happy and excited about that. The man told my dad, "Do this project with your daughter like you promised. Make it beautiful, just like sobriety, one simple step at a time." I thought what he said to my dad was beautiful, but my dad had a different opinion. My dad screamed, "Get the fuck out of my house with your self-righteous bullshit! No one tells me what to do with my daughter!" My dad's sponsor shook his head and walked out of our house. Afterwards my dad threw some things around the house, yelling at everyone and no one, and walked out the front door. I didn't see him for four days.

With love and care that 1957 Mercury could be restored, but no one ever goes beyond talking about it to actually restoring it. The promises are full, but my parents' ability to fulfill them isn't. This cycle never ends and there seems to be no end in sight. I may as well create my own ending because nobody seems to be able to offer me a solution that lasts. I know where to go to get some weed and alcohol, but I'll still wake up somewhere and have to come back to this. I need something permanent, something lasting. Yeah, I'm going to kill myself. I have to go.

Words are spirit without boundaries. Some calling songs aren't sung at ceremonies of life and renewal. Some calling songs are sung in quiet desperation from within the broken hearts of our youth. When she said the words "I have to go," her calling song of pain and desperation was heard and felt by her grandmother in the spirit world. Grandmother looked around for the location of the voice, the very dear, precious and familiar voice of her granddaughter. And so of course her grandmother answered the calling song of her beloved granddaughter.

I've thought about suicide many times. For how many years? I don't know. It feels like I've thought about suicide every day since my grandmother passed on. The only thing that actually scares me at this moment is that I'm not scared. Just knowing I'm going to follow through on this final conclusion makes me feel—well, it makes me feel like my grandmother used to make me feel: comfortable. When I was with my grandmother I knew I belonged, not just with her but no matter where I was when I was with my grandmother, I was home.

Granddaughter, I am here. I followed your voice and now I am here. When you were born I promised that I would always look after you and take care of you. I watched you grow and I gave you strength and courage, but I had to leave. I grew old and it was my body that failed, not my love and desire to be with you. I am here even though you can't see or hear me.

Before my grandmother passed on, whenever my parents would fight, disappear, go to rehab, or get locked up in jail, CPS or the police would take me to her house. Other times I would just walk across the ravine, pass by the tree at the top of the hill, then walk down the hill to her house.

I remember those days. You would run into my arms and hold me so tight that I couldn't breathe. We wouldn't talk about what happened, but we'd pretend that we were on vacation. When you went to sleep, I would cry. I would cry for your mother and father. They love you, but they have not learned how to love themselves. I never cried for you because I believe in you. You have a will to live.

Depending on the time of day, I would watch the eagles that have a nest in that tree on top of the hill before I continued to my grandmother's house. Just that walk made me feel better because I knew it would get me into my grandmother's arms. That's gone now and has been for years. I still go to the tree on occasion to sit, cry, pray to the Creator, and sleep.

All those times and nights that you would sit under the tree, I sat with you. Those were wonderful nights. Sometimes I would go to the tree and wait for you. I would see you crying and knew you were hurting and confused. I would put my arms around you to comfort you and you always felt better. Now it's different. I can't reach you. You left me, you stopped talking to me, you stopped believing in me, and you stopped believing in yourself.

Like tonight, there have been many times I was woke up with the yelling, breaking glass, police sirens, and police radios. Still half asleep, I made my way out of my window and started walking to my grandmother's home. As the cool night air fully woke me, I would sit in our backyard and cry when I remembered that my grandmother wasn't there anymore.

That's not true. I am here. Talk to me.

Isn't it interesting that sometimes we forget people have passed on, and when we remember, it feels just like the day they passed? I wonder if my parents will feel that way about me after tonight. I've only seen them react that way when they wake up in the morning and there's no alcohol, pills, or weed. The broken, bloody mess around the house, and me, the child who had to witness and hear the horror of what happened the night before, are completely overlooked in their search for more booze, pills, and dope. Maybe they need these things so they don't have to face the reality in our home, or maybe these things are the cause of the reality in our home. Either way, I'm leaving this reality for whatever reality is beyond this one. I'm going to walk to that tree where the eagles live and hang myself from it. It's the perfect place for me to kill myself. It's halfway between my home and what used to be my grandmother's home. Halfway between heaven and hell.

Granddaughter, it pains me to see you so confused, hurt and lost. Please take a breath and think. I know you can no longer feel my spirit or sense when I am with you because your heart and mind are filled with so much anger and pain. The anger and pain has filled you and left no room for love, hope or me. I can't comfort you like I used to because you won't let me in. You have forgotten me in memories and fail to realize I am here with you. Don't just trace the memory of me backwards, trace it to me right now. You are thinking and talking so much about me because I am here with you. Whenever you think about someone you love who has passed on, that's when they're with you, offering hugs, love and comfort. Yes, remember me so you remember I am here right now. Memories of all the time we spent together. Memories of all the silly hairdos we created, and the funny dances we made up. The memories are important; they will give you strength, courage and comfort. Please don't be mad at me. I had to go, it was my time to take my new journey. Granddaughter, it is not your time, it is not your time to leave your body, your earthly journey is not complete. You are still creating your memories and your life.

Okay, I'm not going out the front door because the police will be here any second. I'll kick the cardboard out of the broken window and leave through there. What do I need? Not much, right? Okay, what do I want? Should I bring a pen and paper to leave a note? No. Who the hell would I leave a note to? I don't have anything else to talk about, anyway. Oh, I know, I'll bring the blanket my grandmother made for me when I was born. Yeah, I'll bring that blanket and a knife to cut a strip off to make the noose. That way it will be like my grandmother holding me, and in a little while she will be.

You remembered our blanket. Now can you feel me near you? I know you know I am near because I saw a glimmer of love in your eyes. That blanket was a part of our little world. I wrapped you in that blanket when I gave you your Indian name. I wrapped you in that blanket when you were sick, and we shared that blanket when we were cold. I would hold you close to me wrapped in the blanket to help you feel safe and protected. Those were great moments in our life together. Granddaughter, I made that blanket for you, only you, and it is filled

with my love, spirit, and dreams of great things for you.
Granddaughter, before you cut your blanket into strips,
remember the stories I told you about the meaning of
blankets in our culture. A blanket represents love and
respect. When a blanket is given and accepted, it means
that love and mutual respect exist. This blanket was
made for you as a reminder of how important you are
and that your life is valuable. It was not meant to be
used to end your life.

All right, jeans, t-shirt, shoes, hoodie, the blanket my grandmother made me, and my knife. I'm good. I have everything I need for the last time I need anything. Yet there was so much I needed before right now. Looking around my room at the trophies and ribbons I won for track, basketball and academics makes me wonder when those things stopped meaning anything to me. I don't even remember when I began distancing myself from the things I once loved. It's like the flavor of life left and I don't know how to get it back. Anyway, I have to focus. Ripping the cardboard off the window frame, I see there's plenty of room for me to get out as long as I put the cardboard on the bottom of the frame so I don't cut myself while I'm climbing out. The broken pieces that remain in the frame sure do make an interesting shape. Now I'm squeezing through without touching any glass. Yes. Got through. No cuts or scratches, not that it would really matter considering my plan for tonight, but I still want it to be on my terms. Shit, at least this can be on my terms since nothing else has been. Standing outside my bedroom window, I feel frozen, not cold but stuck, like I don't want to move in any direction. What is this? What am I waiting for? I have my plan and everything I need to fulfill it.

You're waiting because you hear me. It is not your time! Today is a good day to live!

Maybe I'm waiting for a feeling to overtake me.

Granddaughter!

Something that will change my belief that possibly the worst thing I can do to myself, my family, and my community feels perfect.

That something is you. You know this is wrong. This is not your destiny, and you know this. Tell your head to be quiet and listen to your heart.

Off in the distance I can see the tree on the hill past the ravine where I'm going to make my last stand. The familiar screams from both of my parents echoing from their battle in the front yard, blending with the sounds of the police sirens on their way to our home, quickly remind me why getting to that tree is perfect. I made it out of the house, so I'm partially free. It's time to take my walk to complete freedom.

Granddaughter, you are so young and innocent. There is so much for you to learn, experience and discover. Complete freedom isn't a destination, it is a work in progress and is earned as part of maturity. Oh, listen to me, you are not ready nor interested in what I am trying to teach you. I love you so much and miss those times when you would let me be your teacher. You always listened and even when you didn't, you pretended to listen, and that's one of many reasons why you are so special. You are going through many changes. Remember times of change can be challenging. And they can also be beautiful, like the fall.

I love fall. This is my favorite time of year. It's a beautiful, clear, star-filled sky. The air is crisp so I can see my breath, but not so cold it makes me uncomfortable. The beautiful colors of the fallen leaves with the full moon glistening upon them looks majestic. They have just enough frost on them to keep me in tune with each step I take, but not so loud that it's a distraction. Walking towards where I will make my final stand, seeing my breath, and hearing my steps reminds me that in a short while my breath and my steps will no longer exist here. The last path I take to a freedom and peace I've longed for, and only found in the arms of my grandmother, will be in the middle of the night, alone, and the trail will be walking away from my home, not towards it.

Granddaughter, we have all gathered, and we are the spirits of the fall, sky, air, colors, and the spirits of all our ancestors. You are never alone and we will do what

*we can to stop you on your path to what you call your
final stand. You are not prepared for your next journey.
The freedom and peace you felt when you were in my
arms was in you, not in my arms. You felt free and at
peace because you wanted to; I did not tell you to be free
and to be peaceful, you chose those feelings and you can
choose them again.*

I need to look back on my home before I descend down
this hill into the ravine. Nervously, I turn around, squeezing
the blanket my grandmother made for me a bit tighter.
Maybe I'm looking for a reason to go back home, or for a
feeling that what I am going to do is wrong. But all I see
are the flashing lights of the police cars coming from the
front of the house, the light from my bedroom shining
through the broken glass, and the faint, yet distinct, yells
of my parents blaming each other for not being there for
me, their daughter.

*Granddaughter, listen to your heart. Your feelings are
real, they are reminding you of the things you already
know about right and wrong.*

Now, squeezing the blanket tightly in my arms and holding it to my face, I can still smell the beautiful scent of my grandmother in this blanket after all these years. Wiping my tears from my eyes with the blanket, I'm not crying for me, I'm crying for what I'm looking at in this moment. The broken windows, the lights from the police cars, the yelling—all transformed to a big ceremonial fire.

Close your eyes and cover your ears, granddaughter. Open up your heart and spirit and listen to the silence. You can do it. Your eyes only see what is in front of them, your ears only hear the sounds they want to hear. Your eyes and ears are only tools for you to gather information, they are your servants and under your control. It is your heart, spirit, experiences and lessons that help you create meaning of all the things you see and hear. Granddaughter, you are so wise, and you are right that what you are looking at in this moment is chaotic and unbalanced. There is yelling, broken glass, loud sounds, bright lights and strangers entering your world. This is real and it is your reality in this moment, but you are confusing it with your destiny and your future.

The yells of my parents are the crackling sounds fire makes when it wants to get your attention, but there's no fire keeper tonight. There's no fire keeper to put some cedar on the blaze, no one to adjust things and make sacred offerings. I guess even ceremonial fires lit with healing intentions can consume us if left untended—unloved. My tears in my blanket are not because my parents are not there for me. My tears are because I will no longer be there for them.

Granddaughter, you are filled with so much love, that's why you are crying. You are not ready for your final stand; you are not ready for the spirit journey. It is not your time. The spirit of the ceremonial fire is calling to you; this is what you know, remember and believe. Granddaughter, you are the fire keeper. You are leaving your fire untended and unloved. I know you are in pain and your thoughts are confusing you, but I have faith in you. You know that when a fire is left untended, it can burn out of control, or it will die. The death of an untended ceremonial fire is a loss of a belief, dream, tradition and person. The fire is your family, the crackling sounds you hear are coming from them, and they're begging for your attention. They're begging you to listen to what is in their hearts.

With one last glimpse upon the ceremonial fire of my home, I inhale the sweet smell of my grandmother, and know I have to continue my journey to the tree at the top of the hill.

Walking down into the ravine, I remember this is one of my favorite parts of the walk to the tree and my grandmother's house. A place of solitude, silence, and a sweet stillness, with only the sound of the small creek I must cross before making my ascension up the hill on the other side to the tree. Across the creek, up the hill and sitting under that tree, I've written many pages of poetry, shed many tears, and visited with whomever was there to listen. I've done a lot of writing, crying and visiting in this ravine, sitting right here by this small creek. The ravine has always offered the same solace for me as the tree on top of the hill. Now I realize this ravine is where I took all the things I needed to unravel before I carried them through the creek for purification, then to the top of the hill to let it all go and gain a new perspective. I must have walked this path hundreds of times in my life. Tonight, my last night on earth, is the first time I've paid attention to the subtle details that made every journey to that tree meaningful.

Granddaughter, you are understanding. You are learning and remembering. Granddaughter, you hold so many sacred lessons in you. You understand the connection between all things. Your tears, the trees, your writings, the creek, the hill and the ravine are all a part of this connection, but there is still more. There truly is a whole world out there waiting for you.

It's fitting that I receive this clarity here in the ravine. Now, it's time to cross the waters of purification to prepare me for my journey. A journey to the embrace of my grandmother, which for me is the only peace I've known.

I can't just jump over this creek tonight. I have to stand in it, even if for just a moment. Wow, that's cold, invigorating, and like my whole being is getting nourished from the water moving through my tennis shoes, socks and feet, blanketing me from within. I love this contrast of the blanket my grandmother made for me covering my outside, while the life-giving water blankets me from within. This is helping me let go. It's perfect. The perfect sounds of the water filling my ears, telling me there will be peace soon, gives me peace now. It's time to carry myself up the hill to the tree. The tree that has meant many things to me throughout my life. The tree that will mean many things to others after tonight.

Granddaughter, we are all with you. The spirit of the water is a strong spirit and is one of the four strongest powers that exist in the universe—water, air, fire and earth. Water is full of healing powers, healing that you're feeling right now. Water is the greatest peace maker. It always takes the path of least resistance but has the greatest strength, and combined with time, it will wear down the strongest obstacle. There is still so much that you have to learn about water, air, fire, earth, and yourself. Your determination to end your life is so strong that you are not hearing what we are saying. Water is telling you that you can always have peace, it is always with you.

My socks and shoes soaked with water now make this easy, thirty-foot climb feel a little more challenging. This climb doesn't feel as free-flowing as the first part of my journey here. I'm feeling the temperature of this beautiful fall night get colder by the second in my feet. I suppose all purification comes with a price, and all prices come with purification. What we're willing to pay, what we're willing to let go of, what we're willing to walk through.

Granddaughter, I am proud that you are remembering so many life lessons. Yes, purification is a very important ceremony, but you are changing the meaning to fit your pain so you can hold on to your pain. Purification is a way to help you prepare for a new perspective and a better way. Do you remember why we have winter? Winter is the purification of the earth. It is the time for the earth to rest and sleep so that it can start anew. The cold keeps everything solid and the snow is the blanket of protection that will soon transform to life-giving water. Purification does not have a price; it's a process, the test of the spirit to let go of what no longer serves you.

This may be the first hill I've climbed in my life for myself. All the other hills I've climbed seem to have been placed in front of me by others. I was willing to walk the journey only to help them with the outcome they wanted to achieve. After climbing the mountains of others, they were happy I did it with them or for them. Me, well, I was tired. I learned some lessons they were supposed to have learned, and the time I spent climbing their mountains took me further from where I should have been walking in the first place.

Granddaughter, the things that you are recalling are choices you made. Every hill, every challenge, and every journey you walked was for you. All these things added to your character.

At least right now I know that every weary, purified, cold, water-soaked step I take is on purpose for me. Just a little further. There, okay, I've finally made it on top of the hill. I love how as soon as you get to the top of this hill it's flat all around. Even though it's only about a thirty-foot-high ridgeline, it always made me feel closer to home. This tree has never looked as good as it does tonight. The colors of the leaves are a mixture of yellow, red and green. Some of the leaves are already blanketing the ground, as if welcoming visitors with the most luxurious doormat that no human could possibly create. Way up top I can see the eagle's nest. The nest is huge, intricate, and beautiful. I don't know if it's because of my purification, or comparisons to what happened at my home tonight, but I've never witnessed the beauty within this tree before. Before tonight, I didn't see it, I just felt it comfort me. It's always been my halfway mark, either heading to heaven, grandmother's house, or heading back to hell—having to go back home. Tonight, it's not a marker or even a place of refuge. I used to look at what I'm about to do as an end, but not anymore. Tonight, this tree is my beginning because my end came so many times before this evening. Check my pocket, yeah, there's my knife. I have to cut a strip off this blanket and make the noose. Grandmother, please forgive me for cutting this blanket that you made me. In a little while we can make a new one together.

Granddaughter, that is what you don't understand, we cannot make another blanket. I am counting on you to complete your journey on earth so we can once again be together when it is your time. You have forgotten me. You have forgotten the lessons I have taught you. You have forgotten the great times we created. Remember me with love. When I died, I didn't die to hurt you or to make you sad. I died because my life on earth was complete. I did what I was put on earth to do, learn and experience. When my earthly journey was finished, I was called to the spirit world because it was my time. That is what you must do: you must live, learn, laugh and experience being a human being. Only the Creator will know when you're ready. You are in your earth mind if you think that you know better than the Creator, and that killing yourself will bring freedom and peace. That is not the truth. That is why you are not ready. What you learn on earth will be your guide to completion and there is no second chance. Granddaughter, I beg you to finish your journey. You will understand why your life is filled with so many unanswered questions and commotion when you're ready. I will not give up on you. You will make a great difference in the lives of many others who need you. I can't reach you because your heart is swimming in fear.

Hey, I cut it pretty straight. I better cut one more strip off to double the noose so it's strong enough to carry me far from here. Okay, made the noose and reinforced the knot with my shoelaces, and put it loosely around my neck. Now I have to find a good branch to tie this to and then test it. I better take my shoes and socks off; something about this seems like I should take off my socks and shoes. Barefoot, yeah, that feels right. Maybe I should have walked the entire way barefoot. No matter, it's time to climb and find a good spot to do this from. Only about fifteen feet up is a good solid branch. Man, I hope the eagles aren't in that nest. If they are, I hope they don't wake up and attack me. Okay, here we go. Easy enough climb, much easier than the hill. Wow! This view is beautiful. Perfect. My last view on this earth is perfect. This is my last view of what I've known most of my life. Let me tie this rope onto the branch; there, that should do it. What's that cracking sound? Oh, no, the branch is breaking.

Granddaughter, do you know when I made that special blanket for you, I knew that I would not always be there for you. I sewed my love, hope, dreams and courage in the fabric of our blanket. My life was filled with challenges. There were many times when I, too, felt my life would be better if I just died. Some days the pain was so great, the words cut like a knife; the actions of others hurt my soul, especially when they were supposed to care for me. I could endure the physical pain, but there seemed to be no end to the emotional pain of those days that felt so very long. I cried, got angry and was sad. I would feel so alone, and it took me years to realize I was never alone. That is why it is so important for you to live. You have not learned all the lessons meant for you, and some lessons will take years. In my moments of greatest sadness, I would take a long walk to the lake through the forest. That is when I realized I was not alone. I would listen to the trees, animals and insects. I would remove my shoes and feel the earth under my feet. Feeling her warmth in the summer and her coolness in the winter, I knew she was alive. I would look to the sky and see the beautiful sun and feel warm in the day, and

at night I would gaze at the stars and feel the coolness
of the night. I would let the pain and disappointment
go and remember I was a strong person. I would dream
about you, and oh what a sweet dream you were, and an
even better reality you are. I would dream that someday
I would hold my grandchild in my arms, and then one
day, I did. I had to live so you could live. I had to dream
so you could dream, but I did not die so you could die. I
will not let you die.

Chapter 2
Dusk & Dawn

"We got another one."

"Roger that."

"This may hurt for a second, sweetie, but we have to do this."

"Keep rubbing her eye until she wakes up."

"I'm rubbing her eye until she goes back to sleep."

"Huh? Why are you two rubbing my eyes? And where's my grandmother? Where am I?"

"Oh, distrust is a lingering feeling. You even brought it here with you."

"Where's here? And who the hell are you two?"

"We're eagles. And you're where you wanted to be."

"You're both eagles? One white eagle and one black eagle?"

"Yes, you can call me Dawn, or the white one if you prefer."

"And you can call me Dusk, or the black one if you like."

"Hello! My name is ..."

"Honey, Dusk and I know your name, we've watched you grow up. Your name is Jessica but over here, on this side, we know you as Beautiful."

"What do you mean you watched me grow up? And why do you know me as Beautiful?"

"Questions can wait for answers, but answers cannot wait for questions. Let's take it slow and really get to know one another. Dawn and I have lots of stories, jokes, tongue twisters, riddles, games, and a whole eternity's supply of leftover bologna sandwiches from spirit plates."

"Dusk?"

"Yeah, Dawn?"

"You said whole eternity."

"Yes, I did!"

"Is that really necessary? I mean eternity can't really be put in parts."

"Every time they drop in like this, they bring memories back of time. My apologies, no partial eternities here."

"Enough, please! You two are scaring me, confusing me, and I really need to understand what's going on. The last thing I remember is a branch breaking, me falling, and then you two were rubbing my eyes with your wings. What's really going on? And please tell me where I am."

"Dawn, you tell her, you're better at this than I."

"Okay, Beautiful, let me explain some things."

"Call me Jessica."

"No! I will call you by what the ancients know you as. I will call you by what the Creator breathed into you. I will call you what you are, Ms. Jessica. I will call you Beautiful, so get used to it, Beautiful. You already got unused to it, now get reused to it. You are in the place where…"

"Come on, Dawn, you can do it, I know you can. No worries, Beautiful, sometimes he gets stuck on this part, but after this he can really tell a good story. Dawn, you got this! Come on, I'm biting my tail feathers off over here. Beautiful needs to know!"

"Dusk, thanks for the support. Okay, Beautiful, you are—well, where do you think you are?"

"I don't know! That's why I'm asking you two boneheads! Heaven? Spirit world?"

"Oh, now I get it. Do you get it, Dawn?"

"No, but since you do, I probably will. Go ahead and explain it to her, Dusk."

"Beautiful, you are in the land of enchantment, the place of nothing and everything, where dreams, hope, love and healing meet eternity and live together in sacred bliss."

"So, I'm dead. Good, that's what I wanted. Now just point me in the direction of my grandmother because that's who I want to be with."

"Dawn?"

"Yes, Dusk?"

"Can we talk for a moment in private?"

"Sure."

"I think that … ha, ha, ha, ha."

"Shhh! She's going to hear us laughing and then she'll really be upset."

"I can't help it, and my sides are hurting from this. Isn't this hysterical?! Ha, ha, ha, ha!"

"Okay, let's just compose ourselves and when we go back over there, if she heard us laughing, let's just say we were singing a song."

"Sounds good."

"Beautiful?"

"What do you two want, besides to make fun of me? I heard you two over there laughing at me."

"*We* weren't laughing at you, Dusk was."

"What! No, I was not! We were laughing at your statement."

"What statement?"

"You said you're dead. That really cracked me up, and the other side of it really cracked Dawn up. You see, Dawn has a fun time talking about the sad things, and I have a sad time talking about fun things. It's not for everyone, but it works for us."

"How can me being dead be funny?"

"Dusk, be gentle."

"I will, Dawn, don't worry. Beautiful, how can you being dead be possible? Do you feel dead?"

"No. I feel light, and a little strange that I'm finding it perfectly normal to be sitting here talking with one black eagle and one white eagle. Nothing seems out of sorts at the moment."

"Okay, so you can see our dilemma. You're here with us. You're speaking with us. You don't feel dead, but you insist on confirmation that you are dead. You cannot die, Beautiful. You cannot kill yourself because you did not create yourself. There's no threat to your existence, only the threat that you won't finish what you were sent to do on earth in human form."

"Oh great, now I'm here in spirit world, and two eagles are trying to make me feel guilty. You two said you watched me grow up! If that's true, then you saw everything that happened to me, right? Everything! And if you two just watched, then I'm angry at you both for not doing anything to help me."

"I apologize, Beautiful, if I came across like I wanted you to feel guilty. We don't use guilt because it's useless. I just wanted you to know that your existence in human form really does mean something to many people, many people you haven't even met yet. Have you heard the expression, *we'll cross that bridge when we come to it?*"

"Yes."

"Well, Beautiful, you've come to it."

"You had a plan to come to this side way before your time—your own way, and by your own hands. Now, I do not want you to feel guilty. And we are aware of what you've endured in your short life. We've heard your cries, we've heard the fights, we've heard the prayers; believe us when we tell you the Creator has heard all of it as well, with perfect clarity. You see, the bridge you are at is a very thin bridge, and since you're here now, perhaps before you continue with your journey to the Creator and then to be with your grandmother, maybe you need to remember some things. I mean, what's a little conversation when you are in a place where time doesn't exist?"

"You two are a trip. And now that you mention it, I did think this side would be different. I thought the second I crossed over here I would know everything, see everything, and feel complete peace."

"Dawn and I have been on this side for what you humans would call centuries. We're still learning and will continue to learn. You humans are in kindergarten; Dawn and I are like in third grade. The learning never stops. Everything you feel and everything you have to face is only amplified in pure spirit form; it doesn't go away until it's dealt with, and that is true for either side. Besides, the sides have many doors, at various times, and you had a plan to choose one this evening. Consider that learning is maybe why you chose to go to earth in human form. To learn some more things and help some more people. I'm not saying it's true for you, just throwing it out there as a possibility."

"What? So, let me get this straight, Dawn and Dusk. You two are centuries-old spirits that talk nonsense, tell stupid jokes, and act like idiots. But you expect me to believe that maybe I chose to come to earth in human form to learn some more things and help some people?"

"Dusk, be gentle."

"As gentle as possible, Dawn. We're not here to coddle you, Beautiful. We don't coddle. We are warriors and ride the razor's edge of what is allowed here. We can spin you around and turn your world upside down. If you think we sound absurd and ridiculous, that is only a reflection of yourself. We are a mirror, and all who enter here will go through a purification before going on with their journey. As painful as it is to look at ourselves, there are no answers outside of this simple step. As Dawn already explained, you are in a place without time, so being stubborn isn't going to help you move on to where you want to go; only honesty will."

"Honesty, huh?"

"Yes, Beautiful, pure honesty."

"Okay, well, here's honesty for you. My life sucks. My parents ignore me. I miss my grandmother because she is the only one who could make sense out of anything, and I desperately want to see her again. I'm sick of seeing fighting, struggles, alcohol, drugs, and systems like family court and child protective services that never seem to end, so I decided to end it."

"Dusk, now I think we're getting somewhere."

"I agree, Dawn, so let's bring it right where we need it to be. Beautiful, can I share a story with you?"

"Yes, if it will help make sense of all this crap for me."

"It most certainly will help make sense of things for you. Besides, every time I tell this story it reminds me of your greatness and keeps me focused on the Great One, the Creator. So, the blessing, as with any blessing, is completely mutual. Before I begin, here, wipe the tears from your beautiful face."

"A rose? You want me to wipe my tears with a rose? Where did you get the rose from, anyway?"

"Oh, we have immediate access to all symbols of love here. Any reminders of the Creator and the sacredness of creation are just a thought away. No different from the way human beings were instructed to live their lives in the beginning, and—well, before the beginning. You see, there was a time human beings strived to live in balance and harmony, which was a constant reminder of the Creator in everyone and everything. That's more than a tradition, it's an instruction, and one given for your own safety and sanity. Besides, isn't it better to wipe your tears with a rose than a tissue?"

"Yeah, it does feel nice. I didn't know there were tears here in heaven?"

"Oh, spirit world doesn't make your world go away. You have to allow it back into your heart, and this is done by allowing the memory, the original dream, back into your consciousness, your immediate memory. And look at you, as soon as you touched the rose to the tears on your cheek, you smiled. That's the first smile you've had since you got here. Isn't it wonderful when someone hands you a reminder of what you really are?"

"You said the rose is a reminder of the Creator, right?"

"Yes, I did. And if something is a reminder of the Creator, it's a reminder of you."

"Yes, I am smiling, aren't I? What is Dusk doing?"

"He's singing."

"Yeah, I know that. But the song he's singing is the song my grandmother sang every morning to start her day."

"Of course it is. Where do you think she learned it from? Not to brag, but we've composed some pretty sweet music. It's heard in both worlds for those whose hearts are open. Do you remember the words?"

"Of course I remember the words. I sang it with her many times."

"Well, you can sing with Dusk if you want and then I'll share the story with you."

"Oh, I would love to …

Creator, because of you, I am here
Creator, you see us
Creator, you hear us

Creator, you believe us
Creator, you accept us
Creator, you have faith in us
Creator, you give us refuge and safety
Creator, you trust us
Creator, you give us peace
Creator, you created us to be of benefit to others
Creator, you love us
Creator, help us to receive all you have given us
So we may give all that You are, all that we are
To all others
And together we may continually sing
To You and all of creation
Because of You, I am here …"

"That was beautiful, Beautiful. Thank you for sharing your miraculous voice."

"Did you hear her? My grandmother. I heard her singing with Dusk and me."

"Of course I heard her. You two sang together before you were even born. Every time you sing, she sings with you. And every time she sings, when you're listening with your heart, you hear her and sing with her."

"You two are pretty cool, and I apologize for calling you idiots."

"Apology accepted. We know you didn't mean it. Even if you did mean it, it wouldn't bother us. We don't get offended because we know there is nothing that anyone can say that will alter the truth of what we are. Sometimes we get hurt that someone would want to offend us, but we hurt for them, not us, because in order for someone to want to offend another, they can't possibly have any idea of the reality of who and what they are, and that is very sad for us see. It should be sad for you humans to see, too. Which leads me to the story I want to share with you. It's our story. The story of the eagles known by all of us on this side. So, are we ready now?"

"Yes, very."

Chapter 3
Eagle Nation Speaks

"Some humans say they know about us. Some say they revere us. Some even utilize us as symbols of freedom, representations of countries, and some say that because we fly the highest of all living beings, we carry the prayers of the people to the Creator. While all these things are good, and some true, it is time for humans to listen to how us eagles view you.

"For too long, our voices have been omitted from the conversations that human beings say are dialogues. While we are claimed as symbols, that reduces us to something in the past. We are not symbols, we are real, and we are here. However, since symbolism is a word that some human beings use, let's look at that. A symbol is something that represents or stands for something else. How can humans strive to embody what us eagles are, what you say we represent, without listening to us? You know it's impossible to know another without listening. I'm sharing with you so you remember what is sacred. And so you regain the same spirit you human beings once had that allowed you to soar. The same spirit that human beings are created in is the same spirit that allows us eagles to soar, and it's a spirit that we, the eagle nation, have never given up.

"We remember everything because we live in a manner that makes forgetting unnecessary. While in the egg, I was cared for and sung to every day by my mother and father. My parents would talk with me and the Creator about their gratitude for my spirit becoming manifest into the physical realm. About a week before I was able to crack through the egg, I listened to my father and mother talking about me. They were so excited and grateful. They sang many songs as they worked, and other eagles would circle our nest and join in the songs of thanksgiving and prayer for me with my parents. In the egg, before my parents could physically see me, and before I could physically see anything, I was given a vision, not of what is to come, but of what I was, am, and will always be—a sacred blessing, miracle and gift. I was seen, heard, believed, accepted. My parents had faith in me and my existence was beneficial to others and the world. There was no darkness within my egg; it was illuminated with love. Many times, while I was within the egg, I thought, *thank you, Creator, for allowing me to be an eagle*.

"When it was time, I broke through the egg and was not only greeted by the light of love that shone from the blue sky, but the light of love that shone through the eyes of my parents. They cleansed me, fed me, and continued to welcome me into the world. Our home was beautiful, and created with everything around that they had access to: grass, leaves, twigs, and even things human beings throw away. There were plastic, wires and paper carefully crafted with love to reinforce our home in the love that created me. In a never-ending gratitude of resourcefulness, my parents utilized all of our surroundings. There was never any lack because love lacks nothing. There were toys waiting for me, along with food that my parents took turns bringing back to our home. All the other eagle families circled around our nest, singing songs of gratitude about my arrival. I went from being enclosed in an egg of love to being supported, high in the tree, in a home of love, and encircled by a community of love.

"All of the other eagle families lived in similar homes because we all had access to the same things. I've heard stories from other eagles who moved to this area from faraway places, and they would share that where they moved from had different resources, so their nests were built with different things, but the nests were always built with love. In love, we build our homes safely, high above the ground, out of the reach of predators. It is the love, not the available resources, that gives us peace and safety. It is the love that allows us to create such beauty out of what some human beings would say is trash. The love and peace that we have, even in times of battle, comes from one simple thing: *we have never strayed from what we are*. We are great because we know, and choose to never forget, that we are created great by the Great One; to think anything less *is* arrogance.

"When some human beings first began feeble attempts to kill all of us, we didn't start thinking that we must be bad or somehow inferior. We didn't partake in human insanity by internalizing violence just because some humans directed it towards us. That was and still is yours, as human beings, to carry or relinquish, not ours. Some humans reported us as almost extinct, but not because we really were. We pitied you and flew to remote parts of the world where our lives and the lives of our children would not be in danger. Then, over time, we returned to certain areas where there was a regained interest in balance.

"We always understood why humans tried their best to annihilate us. It's way too simple for humans to even see. The same reasons why some humans have attempted to annihilate us are the same reasons humans have attempted to annihilate almost every messenger the Creator has sent—the illusion of separation. In every culture, spirituality and language, there exists the truth of *one*. *One Creator, one* heaven, *one* earth, *one* humanity, *one* blood, *one* life, eternally intertwined, connected, and perfected in the perfect love of the Creator. Love created you, me, and all of creation just like Itself. There was a time when all languages, cultures, songs and dances celebrated *one*, by living in a manner of seeing the Great *One*, the Creator, in *everyone*.

"The real warriors, warriors of love, protected and continue to protect the truth of *one*, while the warlike, bloodthirsty, and ego-driven are always attacking or defending the illusion of separation. Anything or anyone that reminds them of the truth of *one*, they seek to destroy. We eagles are a reminder of *one*, and it took a human law to be passed for the fearful to stop killing us. But human law cannot change the fear that always enters the hearts of those who think they are separate. The humans who believe in the illusion that it's possible to be separate also believe it's possible to destroy what is indestructible. Attempts to destroy all memories of *one* lead to a desire to numb yourselves with drugs, alcohol and violence in every form, and these are weak attempts to make the madness of the illusion of separation comfortable. Think about the madness, Beautiful, but only to remember the truth of *one*. It's madness to think separation is even possible when you, all human beings, all of creation, know deep within your heart and spirit that you are not apart from anything, but are a part of everything."

"Hold on, Dawn. I've heard teachings like this before. I know the things you're telling me."

"Do you?"

"Yes, my grandmother shared a lot of the things you're sharing with me."

"So, do you know the teachings, or do you know *about* the teachings?"

"What's the difference?"

"Living them versus just talking about them."

"Dawn, it's really difficult to live those teachings in the world."

"Beautiful, it has become really difficult to live in the world because many are not living these teachings."

"Okay, fine. I understand most of the things you're telling me, but to be honest some of it sounds very judgmental. Isn't putting people in categories of *warlike* and *bloodthirsty* because of their illusion of separation kind of harsh?"

"Beautiful, you are so compassionate and that's why your calling is so great. You have so much compassion for your family, community and ancestors. Let me ask you a question: is there anything more judgmental than imposing a death sentence upon yourself?"

"I...Uh...I guess not."

"You guess not, huh? You look beyond the insanity in other people and see the goodness, the greatness, and the Creator within them. You even do this with those who have deeply wounded you, forgiving them many times over, yet you are unwilling to gift yourself in the same way. You must start including yourself in your own compassion. You used to include yourself in your own compassion; that's how it developed so strongly towards others. That is just one of many things you learned from your grandmother. Do you believe in unicorns?"

"What?"

"Do you believe in unicorns?"

"I don't know. Why?"

"Because there's one behind you."

"Really? Where?"

"I'm just kidding; it was a squirrel. Apart from some of the pictures you've drawn, I've never seen a unicorn."

"What do unicorns have to do with anything you've been telling me?"

"Absolutely nothing, but I would really like to see one. So, back to this whole judgmental thing you brought up. Do you think an eagle would look down on a wounded rattlesnake and decide to take the rattlesnake into the nest to nurse the snake back to health?"

"No, of course not."

"Why?"

"Because the rattlesnake would kill the eagle and the eagle's family."

"Is that judgmental?"

"Yeah, I guess so."

"No, it's not. Judgment is permanent, a from-now-and-forevermore kind of thing. The Creator is the only One Who can accurately judge, because the Creator is the only One Who created. So, the Creator doesn't need to judge, the Creator *knows*. Even when humans stray from the original teachings, move into the illusion of separation, and become fearful and violent, what the Creator made will always be, and the errors that human beings make in their illusions can be corrected. I think the word you are looking for is *discernment*. Discernment is an understanding given by spirit in order to keep balance. There's nothing negative about realizing the nature of something and not allowing it into your mind, heart and home if you know it is destructive. That would be like saying we eagles are so judgmental because we come across wounded rattlesnakes and don't help them. That's laughable and ridiculous. We are aware of their nature *and* their sacredness. The surety of our discernment is based in the knowing of who and what we are. We are not susceptible to emotional manipulation by predators. A fine balance is within us and available to human beings as well. Looking upon even the most violent of persons, but being able to see a son or daughter of the Creator, is the point. Discernment is also being able to look upon yourself with the same sacred insight. We eagles will fight to protect our family and our home, but never because we hate ourselves. We never run from ourselves, so we can see everything else as a part of us. If eagles acted like many humans, we would have forgotten how to fly centuries ago.

"Beautiful, I know you have many questions. But ponder some questions I would like to ask you. Why did your life cease to be a prayer? Do you realize that when you decided others can't change, and nothing will change, you imprisoned yourself? Do you realize, when you decided that playing is bad, or that you outgrew playing, that actually stunted your growth? How is it that you can turn on a computer and see your own home from space, but you stopped taking an interest in looking within your own heart?"

Chapter 4
Intimacy =
Into Me I See

My beautiful granddaughter, Jessica, you are on the bridge to cross over. You have met Dusk and Dawn. I know you can hear me now because you think that you are dead. You think that everything is perfect and that you will find me, but that is not so. Your heart and your spirit are still alive in the human and earthly way. You are stuck between two existences and now it is your choice to remain stuck, return to your earthly journey, or go forward into a world of confusion and unlived experiences. You still think that this place is filled with peace, yet you carry anger and pain, and won't allow love and peace into your heart.

Dusk and Dawn have chosen to be at the bridge and have remained there for centuries. They love confusing people. They love toying with the hearts and the minds of all and telling their story. Their purpose is real and they are there to remind you that there will always be changes and choices in the universe, a universe that includes heaven. In life there is black and white, dusk and dawn, night and day. There is no love without pain, happiness without sadness, balance without unbalance, peace without chaos, and there is no heaven without hell. In order for anything to exist it must have opposition—something to hold it in place. That is why you exist. In order for me to exist, you have to exist. Every grandmother needs a grandchild, otherwise there is no grandmother. I need you to live, but the choice is yours.

"My grandmother is speaking to me. Why can't I turn around to follow her voice?"

"Beautiful, your grandmother always speaks to you, but you don't always listen. There are boundaries here that you cannot cross until it's time and only the Creator can say when that time is. Yes, you can hear your grandmother, but, more importantly, did you hear what she just told you about Dusk and me?"

"Yes, I listened."

"Good. I think it's time we have *the talk*."

"What do you mean, *the talk?*"

"I think it's time Dusk and I talk with you about sex."

"Sex! Seriously. You've got to be kidding. I already know what sex is."

"Oh, really. Okay, if we don't provide you with any new information on this topic, we will stop talking about it, deal?"

"Deal."

"All right, Dusk, you go first."

"Dawn is right, Beautiful. This is a very important topic and one that humans know very little of. I mean, you humans used to, but as with many things, so much has been forgotten. Sex is the highest form of communication two human beings can have. When human beings have sex, their spirits are literally intertwined. Isn't it interesting that two human beings can be willing to intertwine their spirits together, which creates an invisible cord connecting them after the act of sex, yet so many human beings are unwilling to share their deepest dreams, hopes, desires and insecurities with one another?"

"Okay, I've never looked at sex the way you're speaking about it. And yes, it is interesting that people are willing to physically hook up, but not share their hearts with one another."

"I'm glad we have your attention, Beautiful. Dawn, please continue where I left off."

"No problem. Beautiful, you used the term *hook up*. We eagles find it interesting that you humans use words to describe things, never understanding how accurate you are, yet you are often unwilling to pause and think about a phrase. That phrase by itself describes what Dawn just said. Sex, intercourse, is not to be taken lightly, just like your life. Your life is intertwined throughout all of creation and there's nothing more intimate than sharing your spirit with another person. You didn't come from your parents, you came from the Creator through your parents. Do you want to know how we eagles *hook up*?"

"How?"

"Dusk, please explain to Beautiful how us eagles *hook up*."

"Gladly. Beautiful, when we eagles find our partner, we dance with them. You humans call it our *mating ritual*, which is a funny term to us. We don't *mate*, we intertwine for life with our partner. When love brings us together, we fly with our partner as high as we can, lock our talons together, and then we fall. We freefall, and right before we hit the ground, we release one another and fly back up as high as we can, interlock our talons, and we freefall again. We do this all day. Sometimes we do it for several days. This is our dance of love, hope, faith and compassion. Intertwined in love, we soar. Intertwined in hope, we hold one another. Intertwined in faith, we fall, never allowing either one of us to hit rock bottom or be injured. Intertwined in compassion, we devote ourselves to the Creator within each other. After this ceremony of love, hope, faith and compassion is complete, we live forever as one."

"That is beautiful. I wish us humans were like that. I wish we allowed love to lead us to one another. I wish we had a ceremony like yours. Life would be so much better if we lived like eagles."

"Beautiful, why do you think Dusk just shared that story with you? Why do you think we are sharing these things with you?"

"Because they're cool stories. And when I learn whatever it is you're trying to teach me, you'll let me pass by and be with my grandmother."

"Oh, Beautiful, that's not why Dusk just shared one of our ceremonies with you. That's not why we are sharing our stories with you. We are sharing these stories with you because you humans used to live in a manner no different from us. You lived in complete balance. Of course, you weren't literally flying, but you soared. Yes, you all soared in love, faith, hope and compassion. You would rise with one another to the highest places where only love can take you, and hold on to love through one another. You held communities together from a wellspring of hope that the illusion of fear could never dull. Your daily walk was a continuous giveaway of gratitude with the Creator and all of creation. Like we told you before, we are eagles and know what we are, so we don't settle for anything less than that which reflects the greatness that's within us from the Great One Who created us. You humans used to understand this. Humans used to live from within the greatness within you, but somewhere along the way, many of you fell into the illusions of fear. Beautiful, you have to remember that fear always lies in lies and lies always lie in fear. Yet, the holy instant you allow love's light to enter, fear and lies leave, and you soar again. You see, Beautiful, the eagle nation and the two-legged have been given the same ceremonies. The difference is that we make sure we live ours. Our ceremonies are not events or moments, or something to use in emergencies; they are life itself. And because we walk, live, fly, build and communicate in this ceremonial manner, we celebrate and honor life, all life, every day. And the greatest honor we can bestow upon you is to remind you of your greatness, of the way it used to be with you, and can be again."

"Dusk, some of what you said is good, but some of it pisses me off. You make it sound as if everything is perfect with you eagles. And if it is perfect for you, then great, but that's not the case with me, or any of us human beings. If it was, then I wouldn't be here right now with you, would I?"

"Dawn, can you please expound on this for Beautiful?"

"Yes, I can. Beautiful, you keep missing the perfection because you expect it to be perfect. Nothing is perfect or imperfect, it's whether or not we perfect it. As Dusk was telling you, we live in love, faith, hope and compassion, but living these important and necessary life-giving virtues means nothing unless we share them by giving them away. Only the Creator is perfect and does perfect things each and every time, right?"

"Right. Like my grandmother's beadwork. Oh, she did the best beadwork around. And for as good as she was at beading, she always made sure there was at least one mistake in her work. Sometimes she would show me her work when she was done with a project and point out where she intentionally placed the mistake. I would ask her if that was the only mistake, and she would share that there were probably other mistakes, but the one she intentionally placed signified that only the Creator is perfect. She would say she wasn't going to look for other mistakes, because that's a twisted way to be. She would tell me to look for the beauty, to always look for the beauty. I miss her so much, and she said ... she would say..."

"Dusk, hand her a rose."

"Here is a rose, Beautiful. It's okay to cry. Get the poisons out. Your tears are sacred, courageous, and purifying. Crying is the first purification ceremony gifted to you from the Creator. Crying releases our pain so we can soar again."

"Thank you. Yes, I remember my grandmother sharing that only the Creator is perfect and nothing we do is ever perfect, but the Creator will perfect it when we give it away in love. I'm starting to remember a lot of things she would say to me since I've been here speaking with you both. It makes me miss her even more."

"Beautiful, thank you for sharing that with us. Sometimes all it takes is for us to talk about what we thought we forgot to remember that we can never forget."

"Dawn, I don't understand. What do you mean?"

"You said the more you talk about your grandmother, the more you remember all she taught you. You said it makes you miss her even more, but it can also remind you that she is always with you. The more you remember her and share what she taught you with others, the more she lives, and the more the two of you live together."

"I do feel a closeness to her I haven't felt in a long time. I thought it was because I am here on this side with you two. Now that you put it that way, I guess I haven't been remembering her, I've just been longing for her. I don't know. I just... I just don't know."

"That's a great place to start. Not knowing is a good starting point. You can't fill a frybread bucket that's already full!"

"That was a stupid joke, Dusk."

"Maybe, but it made you smile. Are our feathers sacred to you, Beautiful?"

"Yes, you know they are. Very much so."

"And your grandmother took you to many ceremonies and powwows, correct?"

"Yes, many. I loved going to ceremonies and powwows with my grandmother."

"Okay, are your ceremonies and dances sacred to you?"

"Yes, of course."

"Beautiful, are the ceremonies and dances events or a way of life?"

"Like you both were saying earlier, they are a way of life, but like I already said, it's hard to live that way on a daily basis in society."

"And as we've already said, it's more difficult to *not* live that way on a daily basis. Dusk, please remind her."

"I will. Beautiful, there are so many examples we can use, but let's take a powwow as an example. For you, powwows are a significant time to meet new friends, catch up with old friends, sing, dance and honor one another. The singing, dancing and visiting are all prayers. Prayer in its purest sense is communing with Creator, other people, and all life, knowing one another as relatives. If there is no relationship, there is no prayer. If there is no prayer, there are no relationships. Powwows are one of many gatherings where human beings unite and carry on the beauty of the culture to celebrate life. The singing, drumming, dancing, food and laughter is an honoring. Honoring the Creator, the ancestors, the future generations, the women, each other, and the warriors.

"During the powwow when an eagle feather drops from the regalia of one of the dancers, everything stops. Everything stops because a fallen eagle feather represents a fallen warrior. The dance arena is cleared of all dancers except for four veterans. The four veterans surround the eagle feather to protect it. A drum is chosen to sing an honor song for the fallen warrior, while the veterans dance around the eagle feather and gently lift the fallen warrior from the floor. Once the honor song is complete, one of the veterans carries the feather back to the person who dropped it.

"Before giving the feather back to the person who dropped it, the veteran discusses the significance of this moment as well as the significance of the feather with the person from whose regalia the feather fell. Sometimes the feather is returned, other times the individual who dropped the feather may give all their regalia away, although giving all the regalia away is not as common anymore.

"This protocol at powwows is a significant reminder of the sacred. For you, Beautiful, our feathers are one such sacred instrument of relationship, prayer, and connection. They are a reminder of a truth that will never be extinguished by attempts of genocide, racism, bigotry, illusion of separation or even death. Our feathers show you that you can leave your beauty behind for others to dance, sing, pray and communicate with long after your physical existence on this earth is complete. Our feathers are also a significant reminder of humility. Although there is no other part of creation that can fly as high as us, our beauty is something we leave with you, not just to wear while you dance, or hold while you pray, but as an offering, a continual reminder of who you truly are. We carry your prayers directly to the Creator, and we also carry the reminder of your greatness.

"When the powwow stops to honor the fallen warrior, the people do so, not because of what our feathers represent, but because of what they are. They are sacred, as is all life. This common event that takes place at powwows is not a protocol but a way of life, a reminder of who you are as human beings, a significant part of the entirety of creation and the Creator.

"Think about it, Beautiful. What if all communities stopped everything they're doing, and with love, surrounded and protected those who have fallen? What if, every time, one of your brothers, sisters, aunties, uncles, parents, grandparents, cousins or friends were honored at their lowest moments? What if you stopped everything you were doing in your busy lives to sing a song of honor for your fallen ones until they're back on their feet, and then you gently deliver them to safety? What if you saw and treated each other as the sacred beings you are, with a knowing that each of you is not merely a reflection of the sacred, but *is* sacred? What if you treated one another and yourselves with the same reverence you treat our feathers? What if we, the eagle nation, left the sacred reminders in the form of our feathers for you to remember and reclaim who and what *you* are, not what we are? This is the way, the way of life, the lifeway your ancestors lived, continue to live and will live forevermore. Even now, in the middle of feeling like you are disconnected, you still have the connection, Beautiful. You truly still have the power."

Chapter 5
Where is the Power?

"What power, Dusk?"

"I've talked enough. It's Dawn's turn."

"If you do still see us as an embodiment of a great power, freedom, truth, and a direct connection to the Creator, that means there's still hope. Something you may find interesting is we still have hope for human beings, regardless of how human beings view or don't view us. Did you know when we look at you, we see you the same way that some of you see us? We see you as an embodiment of great power, freedom, truth, and a direct connection to the Creator. We see you that way because we are in relationship with all that is, no different than you. That's not to say we don't make mistakes. Everything in creation learns and grows as long as it stays balanced and teachable. Teachings can only be as impactful as the person receiving them is teachable. You've developed a lifestyle on earth that makes forgetting necessary, because in the brief moments when you pause to remember the truth of *one* within you, the Creator and all of creation, you feel as if you've strayed light years from your essence. The truth is that it took just one thought for you to stray from your essence. It only takes the same amount of time to remember your original thought to get back to balance so you soar again. This millisecond in what you call time is all that is blocking you from yourself, yet you treat it as a divide so great where those who attempt to cross it will surely perish. The truth is that those who don't cross this short divide perish in a cycle of illusions they chase, because they never find peace no matter how many pieces of illusion they pick up. You humans don't have a long way to go, you only have seventeen inches to go, and that seventeen-inch journey is from your head back to your heart. Now, can you please take that noose you made off your neck?"

"Yeah, sure. I didn't even know it was still there."

"Okay, now place it on the ground, and make a straight line with it right in front of you."

"Okay, done."

"Here's one of my feathers. Place my feather on the left side of the line you made with that strip from the blanket your grandmother made you."

"Dawn, I thought that your feathers aren't supposed to touch the ground."

"Beautiful, I assure you this is sacred ground. Just do it."

"Okay, there."

"Now, just for good measure, here is some sage, sweetgrass, pollen and tobacco. Place these medicines on the same side of the line with my feather."

"All right."

"Dusk, do you have the props?"

"Right here, Dawn. Do you want me to put them on the right side of the line?"

"Yes, please."

"What are you doing, Dusk? That looks like a bottle of booze, some drugs, a gun and some bullets."

"Beautiful, they're not real, because that kind of stuff isn't here or allowed here. They're just very realistic props, nothing more."

"Okay, but I have no idea what you two are doing."

"Yes, you do. You know what we're doing. It's just a matter of remembrance, that's all. Now, please tell Dawn and me which side has the power."

"Dusk, what do you mean?"

"On the left side of the line, you have one of our feathers along with sacred medicines. And on the right side of the line, you have drugs, alcohol, a gun and some bullets. Which side has the power?"

"The right side has the power. I've seen many people lose their lives to the right side. Yeah, the right side is the one that has the power."

"Yes, Beautiful, you have seen many people lose a lot from the things on the right side. And it's true that drugs and alcohol by themselves have possibly taken more lives than all wars combined. Yet, have you known people whose lives were completely changed and saved by the Creator through the things on the left side?"

"Yes. I have many family members and some friends whose lives changed when they put the drugs, alcohol and violence away and picked up the sacred medicines to live a different way."

"Okay, Beautiful, you've seen the power that drugs, alcohol and violence have, yet you've also witnessed the power the sacred medicines have. Be it the right side or the left side, reach down and pick up that which you think has the power."

"Like I said, I have seen way more people whose lives have been ripped apart by alcohol, so yeah, I think the alcohol has the power. There, I picked it up, now what?"

"Dawn, please tell her."

"Beautiful, *now* that bottle of alcohol has the power. It didn't have any power until you picked it up. Before you picked it up, it was just sitting there. Have you ever known anyone who went inside a store while they were sober, walked past the area where alcohol is sold to buy a soft drink, then left the store and killed someone while driving drunk?"

"No."

"Of course you haven't. For someone to be drunk, they have to pick up the bottle of alcohol and then drink it. Alcohol, drugs, guns, and all the other dream-killers in the world are just lying around. The sacred medicines are also available. Nothing from either the right or left side of the line you are standing upon has any power until you pick it up. So, if they don't have any power until you pick them up, where is the power?"

"With ... in ... me."

"Yes! The power is within you. Like the line in front of you that you made as a noose to kill yourself with, there you stand, always with the options of that which brings life and goodness, or that which brings death and destruction. Every day you're standing on the line of choices. Like the blanket your grandmother made you to keep you warm and comfortable, you used it that way for many years. You wrapped yourself in the wisdom she shared with you and wrote many stories and poems. You sang the songs she taught you. Then, today, you stood on the line of choice and decided to use what was given to you as comfort and healing and transform it into an instrument of death. That is quite the opposite from us eagles, because we always use everything around us for life, not death. From the moment you wake up, you choose. You choose what you're going to think, pick up and allow within your mind, heart, body, emotions and spirit. We assure you, Beautiful, that you're alive to be a healing force, not a destructive force, yet that which you pick up is what you give your power to, and that is the power that will be exercised. At every moment you have the power to choose that which is from the right or left side of the line—the line of choices. And if you have the power to pick something up from either side, what do you also have the power to do?"

"If I have the power to pick it up, then I also have the power to put it down."

"Yes! So what are you going to do, Beautiful?"

"I'm going to put the alcohol down and pick up the sacred medicines."

"Beautiful, if three frogs are on a log and one makes a decision to jump in the pond, how many frogs are still on the log?"

"Two."

"No, three. One just made a decision, but he didn't do anything. He didn't act."

"Okay, okay, I get it. There, I put down the alcohol and picked up the sacred … I picked up the sacred … medicines … Do you hear her?"

"Who? Your grandmother?"

"Yes, I hear her. She's singing and talking."

"She always is, Beautiful. She talks with you all the time, and you hear her and the Creator very clearly within your heart when you pick up the sacred like you just did. Beautiful, see how one choice can change your life?"

"This is the closest I've felt to my grandmother in a long time."

"Beautiful, there's never been any distance between you and your grandmother."

"Dawn, Dusk, I feel ashamed of wanting to end my life. I know that's not the right thing. I need to make it right. How do I make it right?"

"Beautiful, there is no shame here. Shame is a useless thing that sprang forth from the madness of the illusion of separation. What you feel is correction, not punishment, and there's a big difference between the two. We learn and grow, that's how we soar. We molt our old feathers that no longer serve us. You humans molt your old mindsets that no longer serve you when you pick up the sacred and walk in love so you can soar again. There were some thoughts that no longer served you that had to go but couldn't, at least not until you put death down and picked up life once more. We assure you that no one is ashamed of you. The Creator, your grandmother, and all of creation are proud of you and honor you as the beautiful one you are. And you already made it right, Beautiful. You always make it right when you choose life, and that is what you've chosen again, not just for yourself, but for your parents, grandmother, grandfather, and those yet to come. And before we participate in your choice, we want you to know a story about the tree that you were going to use to take your own life. Is that okay?"

"Yes, of course it's okay. I want to hear it."

Chapter 6
The Sacred Tree

"Okay, just lie down, relax, close your eyes, breathe, hold onto the feather and sacred medicines you picked up, and listen. This story has been passed down through many First Nations communities in what is now known as Canada. There were three different groups of travelers walking along the same path at different times. Each of the groups of travelers carried offerings with them.

"The first group of travelers came upon a tree they recognized as poisonous. Because they recognized the tree contained some poisonous elements, they motioned for everyone to go far around the tree, which they did. The first group of travelers offered *avoidance*.

"Days later, the second group of travelers encountered the tree. They, too, recognized the tree contained some poisonous elements. This group saw the tracks of the first group that went far around the tree. The second group of travelers decided to tie a blue cloth to the tree to warn future travelers the tree was poisonous. The second group of travelers offered *labels*.

"A week passed when the third group of travelers came into the vicinity of the tree. They saw the tracks that went far around the tree, as well as the blue cloth warning them the tree was poisonous. The third group also recognized the tree contained poisonous elements. But after much prayer and contemplation, the third group of travelers decided to make their camp around the tree. The tree became the center of their camp and they shared an entire season with the tree. They learned the poisons the tree contained could be transformed into healing medicines when cultivated with care, patience and love. The medicine the tree produced cured sicknesses that once had no cure. With honor, they approached the tree, and with equal honor they parted ways with the tree. Before they left, the group sang a thank you song and tied a red cloth under the blue cloth, marking the tree as holy—a significant reminder of the truth that heaven and earth are forever connected by the sacredness within all living beings. The third group of travelers offered *relationship*.

"Because of the great courage only love can provide, the third group of travelers left tracks that many others have been able to follow for healing. Because of love, the tree is no longer avoided or labeled, but sought for its truth of healing.

"Beautiful, this is a story your grandmother told you many times when you both sat under the tree you were going to use to end your life. Your grandmother always reminded you that the highest level of thought comes from the depths of our hearts. If it's not from the heart, it holds no relationship to anything real. What we offer others, we offer ourselves. When we see healing, be grateful and certain it was cultivated. When we see poisons in others or ourselves, be equally grateful and certain in the choice of miracles by choosing the sacred. Only love knows how to cultivate healing. When we're willing to offer and receive love, we find within ourselves and others the answered prayers, purpose and miracles that have been with us all along."

"I haven't thought about that story in a long time. Yes, she shared that story with me many times. It is one of my favorites. Thank you for reminding me. Dawn? Dusk?"

Chapter 7
Healed Nest

A cool, comforting breeze, which holds the scent of my grandmother, caresses my face as a bright light causes my eyes to flicker open. Standing over me is Grandpa Joe. He isn't my grandfather by blood, but I call him that out of respect. He is the spiritual leader of our community. Through his beautiful, comforting laughter, Grandpa Joe smiles, "Grandchild, it appears you went on quite a journey last night. I'm sure you have lots of stories to share with us when you're ready."

I sit up and look around. Sitting under the tree with my grandmother's blanket—wrapped up with something in it—lying next to me. I see the branch that broke lying next to me as well. My mom and dad run over to me, kneel down, and embrace me as we laugh and cry together. Grandpa Joe is facing the east, watching the sunrise. He's singing the morning song my grandmother always sang. The same song I heard and sang just moments ago when I was still in the company of Dusk and Dawn.

Rising from the ground with some help from my mom and dad, we walk over to Grandpa Joe and begin to sing with him. Our voices blend with the breeze, the sunrise, and the two eagles singing as they circle over us while the first day's light reflects off their beautiful wings. As I look up at the eagles' nest in the tree, I see the strips I cut from my grandmother's blanket. Those strips are now carefully wrapped around the eagles' nest. The eagles took the noose and used it to fortify their home. In their great love, the eagles took what was going to be used for death, unraveled it, and used it for life.

Grandpa Joe finishes singing. "Grandchild, eagles know how to transform even the worst of poisons into healing medicines. Eagles know how to make a home from anything, because they've never left the home within their own hearts. Since you walked back to your own heart last night, perhaps you'll spend the rest of your life helping others to do the same. Beautiful, yes, that's your real name. I have a feeling you'll spend the rest of your life reminding others of their own beauty."

Surprised that Grandpa Joe called me by the same name Dusk and Dawn did, I ask, "Grandpa Joe, how do you know that they called me Beautiful?"

"Grandchild, do you think you're the first person that's come to this sacred tree of life out of pain, frustration and desperation? I came here when I was your age with the same plan you had last night, because of the same overwhelming pain you've carried far too long, just wanting the pain to stop. I, too, met Dusk and Dawn. After my time with them, and being given a second chance and allowed to return, just like what you experienced, I've spent the past sixty-five years going everywhere the Creator has sent me, sharing the message they gave me to share. And in sharing the great message I was given, some have still chosen to take their own lives, but we'll never know how many have made the choice to hold on, stay, and live. And it is for those we've lost, those with us now, and those yet to come, that you must continue sharing the message that will unravel pain, hurt, and trauma to create a space of healing, joy and miracles, just like the eagles did with the noose that's now being used for comfort, safety and protection."

"Grandpa Joe, what message? I don't have a message. I'm only fifteen years old and even if I did have a message, no one is going to listen to me."

"Grandchild, some people your age and older than you may not listen to you, but some will. And many who are younger than you will definitely listen. Sharing the great message given to you by the Creator is not about who won't listen or who refuses to listen, it's about those who do listen, who will listen, and there will be many more than you'll ever know. Your job isn't to know how many people listen or how many people the great message will help, your responsibility is to share it wherever Creator sends you."

"Grandpa Joe, what message?"

"Grandchild, walk over to the tree of life and carefully unfold the blanket your grandmother made for you. What's inside the blanket is the medicine, the great message you're going to carry with you to remember, to remind countless hearts and minds that we, all human beings, need one another. And how to be there for one another, so that we choose life and that people will live."

Walking towards the tree, I begin to feel shivers, not bad ones, but the kind you feel when you're in the presence of something powerful, something sacred. I kneel down in front of the wrapped-up blanket my grandmother gave me. I know my life will change the minute I unwrap the blanket, so I hesitate for a moment, look up at the top of the tree, and watch the two eagles peering over their nest, looking at me as if they want to make sure I take this next step. I begin to hear the song my grandmother sang, not with my ears, but with my heart. Through the song my grandmother sang, I can hear her beautiful voice whispering to me ...

Granddaughter, open this sacred bundle that Dusk and Dawn have gifted you to fully open your heart once more to the love of the Creator, the love that created you exactly like Itself. Share the message and your beautiful heart with the world. People will listen. People will choose to live because you've chosen to live. Share love. Share life.

Reaching out towards the bundle, I feel warmth emanating from it and begin to gently open it. As I open it, I feel the pressure and tension leave my body, and I am at peace. With the blanket fully spread upon the ground in front of me, I see one white feather, one black feather, sage, sweetgrass, cedar, pollen, cornmeal, and tobacco. Between the two feathers and the medicines is a rolled-up birch bark scroll. I sit in awe at the beauty of what's within this bundle and the feeling of peace and love that is emanating from it.

"What you're feeling right now, granddaughter," Grandpa Joe shares, "are the same feelings your mom and dad had when they saw you come into this world for the first time. Those are the same feelings your mom and dad feel for you each and every day, even during those times when they're not able to express those feelings. What you're feeling right now are the same feelings your grandmother had for you when you sang, cried, and played with her. Your grandmother placed those same feelings you're feeling right now in the blanket she made for you. The warm, pure feelings of peace and love that you are feeling right now are what we can all feel about ourselves and one another when we look at ourselves and one another as the Creator sees us. Open the scroll and read the message, Beautiful. A message that will help all of us see again."

Slowly opening the scroll, as I see the first six words I quickly roll it back up and feel overwhelmed. "Grandpa Joe, who is going to listen to me share this?"

My mom and dad, holding hands, walk over to the tree, sit down in front of me and the sacred bundle, and lean back on the tree. My mom whispers, "We will, Beautiful. We'll listen to the message you've been given to share. We'll listen to everything you want to share with us from now on."

My dad, with tears streaming down his cheeks, pleads, "Jessica, your mother and I threw away all the alcohol and drugs. Grandpa Joe gave me back my prayer bundle that I gave him a long time ago because I didn't feel worthy to carry it. He also said that by morning you'd have your own prayer bundle as well. Last night, when he asked us to pray with him, I told him I didn't feel worthy to approach the Creator because of the choices I have been making for many years now. He asked me a question that brought me back to myself, which of course brought me back to the Creator, you, and your mother. He asked me if I use soap when my hands are clean or when my hands are dirty. Of course, I said, 'When my hands are dirty.' Then he just sat there, staring at me, until I got it. And I got it. I get it now. Our home, minds, bodies, spirits, and emotions have been cleansed and purified. It's for real this time, baby girl."

I sit there, staring at the sacred bundle opened up before me, not knowing what to say to my parents because it has been so long since I've heard them talk like this. My mom pleads, "Jessica, I know you've heard a lot of promises many times over from your father and me, but he's right. This time is for real. I know it. I feel it. We're not saying that we won't have our challenges, but together, as long as we keep picking up the sacred and lifting each other up in prayer and love, we can get through anything. Do you believe us, Beautiful?"

I can hear my grandmother speaking to me again.

Granddaughter, what Grandpa Joe has told you about the sacred bundle and the great message you've been given to share is true. The first people who need to hear the great message are your parents. You've already opened up the sacred bundle. Now open up your heart, unroll the scroll, and share the important reminder with them and the warmth of the peace, love and healing of those words.

"Mom, Dad, I believe you. I've always believed you and I always will. I just wanted the pain to end, not my life, and I'm grateful my life didn't end. I'm also grateful that a new life, a new beginning, is happening for us. I love you both. Now, as I read the words written on this birch bark scroll, we'll remember together, heal together, and soar together, for ourselves, our family, our community, and the world."

As I pick up the scroll and unroll it, looking up to the sky, I ask the Creator to help me read it clearly and bless the words as they're spoken so they bring healing to those who hear them. I know this great message is being spoken through me by the Creator, the ancestors, and those yet to come. Spoken for all of us still here, to remind us that we need to love and support one another so that we choose life, and so that people will live.

Because of You, I am Here

***Until someone sees you as a sacred blessing,
miracle and gift, they have not seen you.***

Although I was told many times that I would be dead or
in prison before the age of eighteen, you didn't see me as a
problem needing to be incarcerated, beaten, or thrown away.

Although I was abused and experienced other traumas
that no one should ever have to endure, you didn't see me
as a victim who, at best, could only rise to mediocrity. You
didn't see me as at-risk, a problem, or mediocre. You saw me
as a sacred blessing, miracle and gift. I knew that, for the first
time in a long time, I was seen. And because you saw me,
truly saw me, I began to see myself.

Because of you, I am here.

***Until someone hears you as a sacred blessing,
miracle and gift, they have not heard you.***

Although I was talked at and talked to most of my life, you
wanted to hear my voice. My voice that had been beaten back

into the recesses of my mind. My voice that I had hidden for so long out of fear that it would be scrutinized, disrespected, mocked, and rejected again. I didn't even know where my voice was when you came to me. Yet, through your ability to listen and skillfully use the power of silence, you walked me through my internal abyss of pain, loss, and tragedy. You shone a powerful light of listening upon the words I thought were lost. You unraveled the voices of strangers, illusions, and lies, gently removing everything I'm not, so I could once again hear my own voice recall and reclaim the sacred blessing, miracle and gift that I am.

You heard me. And because you heard me, I began to hear myself.

Because of you, I am here.

Until someone believes you as the sacred blessing, miracle and gift that you are, they have not believed you.

Before you came to me I had made many outcries, none of which were ever investigated. I was not advocated for. I wasn't believed. So, I began to follow the three rules that exist in all unhealthy relationships: Don't talk. Don't tell. Don't feel.

These three rules amount to nothing more than suppressing our truth, but I followed these three rules to where they always lead us: bottles of alcohol, drugs, putting ourselves in harm's way, and suicide attempts. But you weren't like the others. You saw me, listened to me, and believed me. You showed me how to talk, tell, and feel.

Because you believed me, I began to believe myself. Because of you, I am here.

Until someone accepts you as a sacred blessing, miracle and gift, they have not accepted you.

Because you saw me, heard me, and believed me, I knew you accepted me. I knew it was acceptance because it wasn't conditional. I didn't have to prove anything. Your acceptance didn't depend upon my attitude, behavior, grades, or what I could produce or consume. Before you came to me, I was around people who accepted me only as long as I followed their rules. As long as I didn't talk, tell or feel, I was accepted. As long as I was willing to not be true to myself, I was accepted. As long as I was willing to harm myself or die, I was accepted. You couldn't have cared less about my willingness to die; however, you were extremely passionate about me regaining a willingness to live.

You accepted me. Because you accepted me, I began to accept myself.

Because of you, I am here.

Until someone has faith in you as a sacred blessing, miracle and gift, they don't have faith in you.

You saw me, heard me, listened to me, and believed me. How could I not know you had faith in me? You didn't just believe me when I told you what was done to me as a child, you advocated for me in the face of those who wanted me to crawl back to the three rules of don't talk, don't tell, and don't feel. You didn't just ferociously advocate for me, you saw what no one else saw, including me. You saw greatness. You knew that you could not have a relationship with my potential, but you knew I could. You uncovered the lies and illusions that blocked me from seeing, hearing, believing, and having faith in my potential. You often said, "As we are dealing with the facts of our circumstances, never take your eyes off the truth beyond the facts. Sure, you can cut an apple open, take out the seeds, count them, and tell me about the number of seeds in the apple, which is a fact. But hold up one of those seeds and ask yourself how many apples are within that seed. The answer to that question is a truth beyond the facts."

You had faith in me, and because you did, I began to have faith in myself.

Because of you, I am here.

Sacred blessings, miracles and gifts are kept safe.

You saw, heard, believed, accepted, and had faith in me. How could I not feel safe? Yet, it was more than a feeling, it was truth. A truly safe place and space majestically appeared whenever I was in your presence. Knowing I was safe made my life easier, and although some days I still tried to push you away, it was only because I felt safe that I dared to push the limits. Because what I learned before you came into my life was that conflict, no matter how miniscule, had one result: violence. The violence could be physical, where someone was beaten for having a bad day, a different opinion, or just saying a little too much. Or it could be the type of violence where someone was ostracized, no longer included, with a shunning that would make a physical beating feel comfortable. Then there was perhaps the worst violence of all, when someone disappeared, not away from you, but right in front of you, a disappearing act where someone who was safe no longer was. With the pop of a pill, the piercing of a needle, the gulp of some wine, a puff of some smoke, or a snort of some powder, then poof! They were gone, and so was my safety. You never forced anything. You allowed me to be. My experience wasn't something you tried to interpret, but something you didn't allow to interpret me. Although our experiences form us, shape us, they don't have to imprison us. The place and space of safety that came freely in your presence freed me. Knowing everything was safe with you—my life, words, thoughts, good and bad days, mood swings, laughter, prayers, love, tears, hopes, dreams and fears—freed me. Your safety freed me from the worst kind of prison: a life sentence, not behind bars, but within my mind. You helped free me so that painful moments of my life didn't become the rest of my life.

You gave me safety, and because you did, I began to feel safe within my own heart, take refuge in my own heart, and live from my own heart.

Because of you, I am here.

We trust sacred blessings, miracles and gifts.

Like you, and most other people, I had given my trust to many who broke my heart. At the time I didn't know why I was giving life and trust another chance. Now I know. When you said the words, "I trust you," it permeated my soul like a life-giving breeze on a hot, humid day. Your trust renewed me. There was no calculated, direct, or indirect threat attached to your trust. You trusted me the same way you respected me, you just gave it unconditionally. And when the time came for me to have some closed-book tests, those times when you told me to make my own decisions, I didn't pass all of them, but you reminded me there's no such thing as failure, only lessons. During my relapses into old habits, behaviors or choices, you kept telling me, "Relapse happens. It's part of this dance and does not mean you failed. I trust you. Besides, life doesn't have to be a closed-book test. Open your heart and receive your answers. You are a sacred blessing, miracle and gift."

You trusted me, and because you did, I began to trust myself. Because of you, I am here.

We give peace to sacred blessings, miracles and gifts.

I could let my guard down with you. I could be me and experience the power of vulnerability, which is a manifestation of courage that can only happen when someone knows they're safe. Your presence provided peace. I didn't know how to react to peace because I was so used to swimming in chaos. I spent so much of my childhood at funerals, in hospital waiting rooms and rehabilitation centers, witnessing car wrecks. Or waking up to glass breaking, to screams and fighting. Or making up excuses to try to hide what the neighborhood already knew. Peace was loud, uncomfortable, and not easy to digest. But with your help, guidance and, most importantly, your consistency, I grew accustomed to peace. No matter where you are now, just knowing that you gave someone the gift of peace should cause you to have more peace to give.

You gave me peace, and because you did, I am living a life of peace, and always looking at how I can better share peace with others.

Because of you, I am here.

We know that sacred blessings, miracles and gifts are of benefit to others, all life, and the world.

Before you came into my life, I didn't think my life was of value to anyone. I was not simply within the grip of self-pity; I was depressed, arrogant and angry. I lived in a constant state of despair and hopelessness, yet you taught me that all my experiences, if I allow them to, can be not only of benefit for me but for others. You taught me that any poison can be transformed into a healing medicine with the right ingredients. You taught me how to transform poisons into healing medicines and that the anti-venom does contain venom, but other ingredients are added to it. You gave me the ingredients of love, faith, hope and compassion and let them run their course. Your ingredients of love, faith, hope and compassion mixed with the anger, false pride, unforgiveness, hurt, pain and loss I carried, until I awoke as a healed, renewed creation, with many tests that have been transformed into my testimony. It is an experience no one can take from me, with a love and gratitude that awakened me to wanting to give all I have been given to others.

You showed me that my life is of benefit to others, and because you did, I live every day to be of benefit, to give all I can. And in this giving I have recognized my true calling by one key trait: That which fills me when I give it away.

Because of you, I am here.

We love sacred blessings, miracles and gifts because they are a reflection of the Great Love that created us exactly like Itself.

I had been told *I love you* in many ways, yet none of them filled me with the undefinable concept of love until you came into my life. I had such a huge void that nothing could fill until you came along.

Little by little, with each time you saw me as a sacred
blessing, miracle and gift,
and each time you heard all that I was saying and not saying,
with everything about me being believed,
and all that I am being accepted,
and you having faith in me,
making a safe space and place,
trusting me,
giving me peace,
and helping me realize that my life is beneficial to others,
the huge thick walls that locked my heart away
came crumbling down, flushed out through
the river of my tears, and I loved again.

I loved again because you loved me. You loved
me, and because you did, I love myself, and
because I love myself, I love others.

Because of you, I am here.

&

Because I am here, I am here for others.

Granddaughter, there are many who do not see the beauty in their surroundings, their life. There are many who wander looking for a place, a person, to give them a reason to live. What you have learned tonight is that the reason to live exists in everything, not just one place or one person. You learned that the path is a journey only you can make, but it's a journey that is never walked alone. All your ancestors, all your relations, the entire universe will walk with you if you let them. Granddaughter, will you let them, will you let me, walk with you?

Beautiful Jessica walked quietly, her smile beaming behind the tears of joy now streaming down her face. "Grandmother, I know you are walking with me. I now know you have always been there. I am sorry I was so sad and angry that I thought no one cared about me. But everyone cares about me. I just need to learn to let others help me build my nest. My nest will be made of strong beliefs, with twigs of love, faith and respect for myself. Grandmother, I will let them walk with me. I will let you walk with me. I am never alone."

About the Authors

Pershlie "Perci" Ami

Pershlie "Perci" Ami is a member of the Hopi/Tewa Tribe, from the Village of Walpi, AZ. As a Hopi elder, coming from a marginalized community, Perci overcame the social, educational, and economic challenges, and has used her struggles and experiences to help others overcome barriers just as she has.

For more than ten years, Perci has served as a strong advocate for suicide prevention, substance abuse, and addiction, devoting her time to the Native American Center for Excellence Substance Abuse Prevention Program as a facilitator for the Gathering of Native Americans (GONA). Perci is associated with the *Voices of the Grandmothers*, which consists of Indigenous grandmothers from all over the world, whose purpose is to share traditional beliefs and stories reflecting a holistic existence of life.

Perci received the Women's Federation for World Peace USA, *Her Story Award*, honoring her exemplary work of serving, healing, educating, and uplifting others in the Native American communities. She also received the Marcus Harrison Jr. Leadership Award for her tireless efforts in advocating for Indigenous peoples with disabilities.

Perci played the lead actress role of Daisy, in the newly released film, "Touch the Water" (2023), which is a movie about the mental, emotional, and physical challenges faced as an elderly Native American woman who desires to accomplish a lifelong goal, which ends up being a life-changing journey, as Daisy is challenged to believe she is never too old to dream.

Perci utilizes her values of culture, traditions, and family in her peace work, helping Indigenous people connect and focus on healing the mind, body, and spirit. When she is not providing her counseling and facilitating services, Perci volunteers her time at a local ministry in Phoenix, serving individuals within the city of Phoenix, and the homeless.

Anthony Goulet

Anthony Goulet is a transformational author and speaker whose writing and work in youth violence prevention and suicide prevention is endorsed by the Dalai Lama and other leaders.

Anthony has been working in youth development for more than 30 years. For more than a decade he was on-call 24/7 as a street-level Gang Interventionist and Street Outreach Worker, serving youth and young adults who were homeless, runaways, missing and trafficked. His full-time office was under bridges, within drug houses, abandoned buildings, and inside emergency rooms delivering the Creator's light of love, hope and healing.